Humphrey Bumpfrey

Sarah Hunt

Ilustrated by Carol Hailstone

ink!
By The Author School

Published in Great Britain by ink! By The Author School 2020

A CIP catalogue for this book is available from the British Library.

ISBN 979-8-6709-6968-0

Typeset by Blaze Typesetting

Printed in Great Britain by Amazon

ink! By The Author School
Kent, England, United Kingdom
Email: inkpublishingservices@gmail.com
Website: www.inkpublishingservices.co.uk
Twitter: @services_ink

Dedicated To

This book is dedicated to my Auntie Joan Broad. We sat and wrote this book when I was a small child.

Thanks To

I would like to thank my supportive husband Michael who always believes me and is always so kind. I love you forever.

Thank you to the lockdown that gave me the time to enjoy writing this book.

My supportive Clients that became friends I could not of done this without every single one of you.

Thank you to the talented Carol who is a famous Nail Artist, for drawing my pictures in South Africa on her lockdown.

The day was dark and cloudy, with a chill in the air. Humphrey Bumphrey was looking out the window of his sweet shop that had been passed down to him from his Bumphrey ancestors. He sighed with a big, catty huff and thought, 'It's quiet, the sweets are not selling, the treacle needs to sell.' Humphrey was worried.

Across the road, in the small village, lived Poppet Moppet. He had a very busy shop selling wellington boots.

It rained a lot in Roggergate so everyone loved his boots, they came in all colours: glowing yellow, purply pink, and glitter rainbow was his best seller. Even the street seemed to love them; it was like the puddles turned magical with the little ones splashing their wellies to make the water sparkle.

Poppet Moppet waved to Humphrey, who was staring at him. Humphrey waved back and turned to look at his treacle wheel spinning, 'Oh, please come to try my treacle wheel,' he thought.

It stood in the centre of the shop like a Ferris wheel in a fairground, spinning lovely, dark treacle for the children to fill their small bellies on.

It was a new idea. It had come to him like a lightning bolt. Although he is still unsure as to how he had made the wheel of treacle: it was like a dream. He made the wheel and made the sugary liquid with such ease in just one night.

Humphrey Bumpfrey shook his head, unable to work out how he had managed it.

He scratched his head whilst he wandered back to the counter to await his customers.

'Good morning Humphrey.' The bell tinkled as the door opened to the shop. 'What a cold day we have today!'

Rolo Polo came bounding through the door wearing his huge coat and carrying his walking stick. He was a funny old poodle; he had big hair meaning his hat did not sit on his head correctly, it was like candy floss. 'I've come to sample this treacle all the village has been talking about! Is it as tasty as my mother used to make? I do hope so young chap.'

Humphrey laughed, "It's better, it's like the sweetest treacle in the world! Here take the little cup and pour yourself a cupful.' He passed him the little cup and spoon. Rolo filled it with delight.

'That's four drogs please, Rolo.'

Rolo gave Humphrey his money and started to spoon his treacle into his chops.

'Well, well, well, that my friend is the best treacle I have tasted, thank you.' He grabbed his stick and left the shop. . .

The bell rang behind him. Humphrey was so pleased. This was a good sign. Rolo had said it was the best in the world, so the whole village would know in no time at all, after all Rolo was the local gossip.

The wind was picking up and rain was splattering hard on the old windowpane of the shop. This was a strange day, something was in the air, he could not tell what it was.

There were dark swirls of grey spinning around in circles like a freshly brewed cup of tea swirling with a sugar cube.

'This was not on the weather forecast today,' thought Humphrey, 'it said on the radio it would be a sunny, dry day.'

Humphrey chuckled to himself, they never usually got the weather wrong, but today they had...

9

'What on earth was that?' Humphrey screamed out loud.

He ran to the window and looked up in the sky to a sight he would never forget in all his cat years…

CRACK, BASH, BANG…

He raised his paws to cover his ears, what on earth… the noise was so loud he almost fell over! He could only see rain; the wind had picked up so much it was like a river falling from the sky… CRASH.

Lightening flew across to Poppet's shop and bolted the wellies on the display right up into the sky. All the glitter wellies were floating about in the sky. They looked rather pretty, but then BAMMMMMMMMM, the biggest, roundest piece of metal landed in the middle of the road.

What on earth was that…? The whole of the shop was shaking like a jelly.

'Blooming heck,' muttered Humphrey who picked himself up and clambered back to see, through the window, the huge massive metal thing was still there with the biggest hole in the road, you ever did see.

Poppet Moppet was hiding behind his welly boots. He was scared to come out of his shop.

There was a sound like an engine trying to start, but it was not of an engine of this world. It was spluttering like Rolo Polo's old cough.

Poppet Moppet opened his door slightly to take a peek at the monstrous object that was stuck in the road. It was well and truly stuck like wellies in thick mud.

He saw Humphrey doing the same, peering out of his sweet shop.

'Humphrey!' he shouted, 'Are you OK?'

'Yes, Poppet, are you? What is that thing?' shouted Humphrey in reply.

'I don't know Humphrey,' Poppet said as curiosity got the better of him and he stepped out...

You would not believe what he saw!

The metal object appeared to have some kind of sticky substance oozing from a silver hole in its side.

It looked a lot like Humphrey's treacle.

There was a crashing noise like pots and pans banging together but on a much larger scale!

KABOOOMMMMMMMM.

With a huge, bellowing puff of smoke a large ladder appeared out of the silver hole. Oh it was very smoky. It was so smoky Poppet had to rub his paws to try and see again, his eyes adjusted and there it was...

Humphrey stood like he was stuck in glue; he had a feeling of déjà vu. Is this a dream?

Humphrey thought that perhaps he would awake in his cat bed very soon, or maybe he had too much cat nip this morning. He felt very funny.

The ladder was now in front of him, smoke appeared, it was foggy and unclear, but he saw a shadow, or two, looming at the top of the ladder.

The two silhouettes were coming down the steps, slowly and unsteadily. Humphrey looked over at Poppet, who seemed to be frozen still, staring at the object. He was clearly afraid too, as his tail was still, he usually had a wagging tail.

Out of the smoke silhouettes started to form a shape, it was the most unusual thing Humphrey had ever seen, but he felt he had seen this before. It all felt so familiar.

There stood two little people, or things, he could not work out which. Humphrey had no idea what they were, but they were brown and had boggly eyes, a huge mouth, skinny bodies and were wearing big, black boots. 'How very odd,' he thought.

They stumbled down the silver object and reached out to Humphrey, 'We need your help Humphrey.'

'How do they know my name?' he thought worryingly.

'We have run out of treacle and crashed to Earth on our way home, we need your help!'

19

'How, how, how, can I help?' stuttered Humphrey. He was shaking like a leaf.

'We programmed into your brain and told you how to make the treacle, you have to get us home. You have the treacle flowing in your shop. We need to get it back in our ship to get home. You are our only hope… we also need a mechanic…' one of the creatures said quickly.

'Ummm, I have the treacle, but I am not sure I have enough for your ship, I will need more ingredients!' exclaimed Humphrey.

'The mechanic is down the road, I will get Poppet to grab him! Poppet… Poppet!' Humphrey shouted.

Poppet was still staring at the object. He slowly turned to look at Humphrey with a surprised look on his face.

'Go get Sparky Malarkey, he must come quickly. Quick, go and get him,' Humphrey shouted.

Poppet turned and ran down the road doing as he was told.

'Where can I get extra sugar? That's what I need to make the extra treacle,' Humphrey thought.

'I know, Mrs Spice the cake maker, at the cake shop… she will have plenty.'

The news was getting around and everyone in the village now stood staring at the unusual object in the middle of the road. It was a small village, so there were only a few people. Rolo Polo was there of course.

'Rolo, grab Mrs Spice, we need sugar…' ordered Humphrey.

'What… what… is that… what… what… are they?' replied Rolo.

'No time for that now Rolo, go and get Mrs Spice, we need sugar.'

'Yes, yes, yes, OK, I am on my wayyyyyy.' Rolo turned around and ran off.

Humphrey knew he would do his duty.

Sparky Malarkey raced to the object, shaking and out of breath. 'What is this? Why am I here? I am scared. What, what are they?'

'Snap out of it Malarkey, we need you to fix the space ship. They have crashed and need treacle to get home, but they have a damaged ship, can you help them?'

'I have tools,' replied Sparky, 'but will they work?'

The lost ones looked at his tool bag and took out a very big hammer and shiny nails.

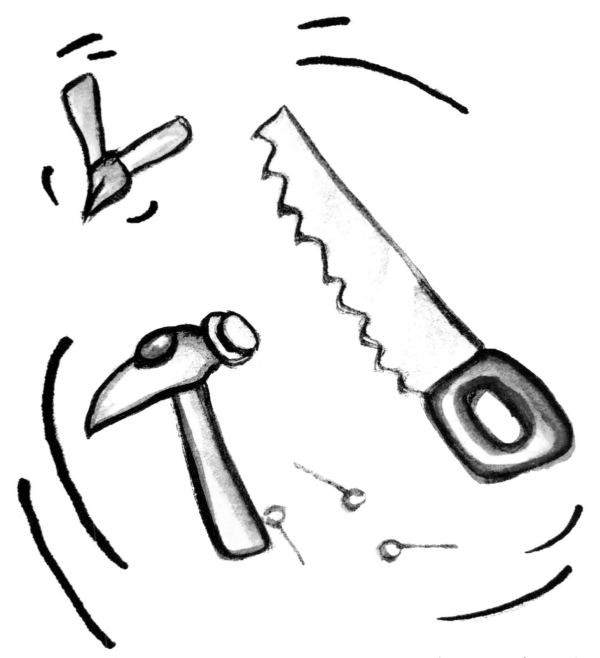

Wandering back up the ladder they began to bash and crash their ship. They threw pieces in the air, nearly hitting Poppet on his head!

'Sorry,' they shouted, before coming back down the ladder. 'No, that did not work.'

Poppet ran to his shop...

Poppet returned with glitter wellies on each paw, they made him look funny.

'Let me have a look, I think I may be able to see what needs to be done.'

He ran up the ship and stuffed the wellies into the gaping hole! They even matched the shiny object.

'That will do it.'

Humphrey gazed up at the glitter boots and where there was once a hole, there was now rubber glitter.

'Thank you, you have helped us so much, now all we need is treacle to get home...'

29

Rushing up the road with her bloomers showing, Mrs Spice arrived, out of breath. She stared at the funny people with a look of shock, her double chin dropped to her chest as she puffed and panted for breath.

'Humphrey, you have all the sugar you need, but how are you going to make this treacle?'

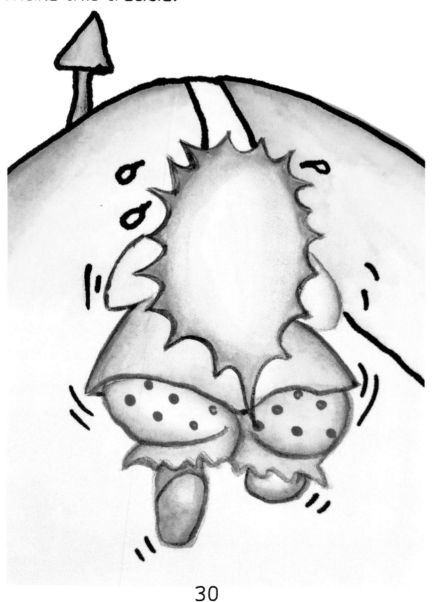

Humphrey had an idea. 'We need a hose pipe, a big tub and fire, then we can heat and pour it straight into the ship. Rolo; grab your hose and connect it to Mrs Spice's sugar machine.'

Off he went to get his hose to connect to the sugar pump.

Now to get the fire going.

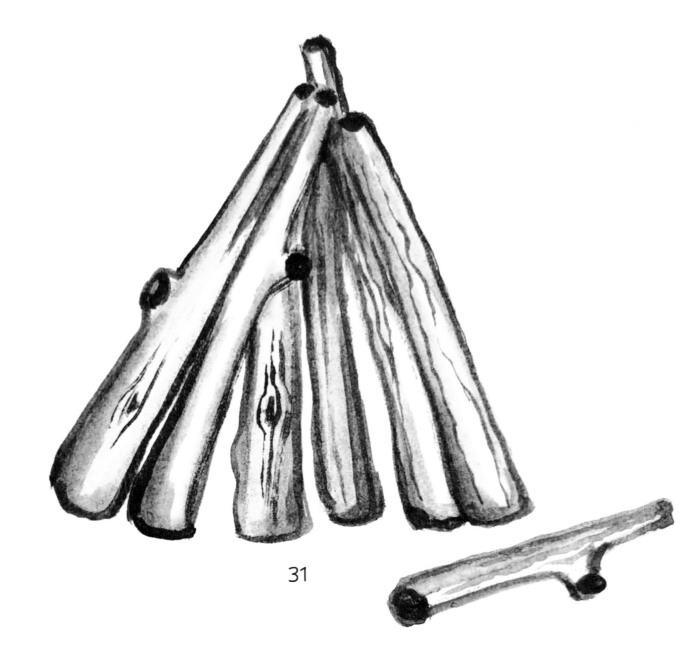

'We need Twix Sticks; he has wood in his shop. Where is he? He must be here somewhere! Twix Sticks are you here?' Humphrey shouted.

From behind the tree appeared a thin tall man. 'Yes Humphrey, I am here.'

Shaking and nervous, Twix listened to Humphrey explain what he must do to make a fire. Twix agreed and off he went to get wood.

The little people were becoming worried, as they had not been to Earth before. They felt the cold.

'We are tired, we want to go home.' Green tears fell to the ground like big blobs of slime.

'Don't worry, we won't be long, we are all going to help you.'

Rolo screamed, 'The pump is ready!'

Twix returned with wood.

Poppet returned with raincoats for the little ones.

Humphrey had an old bath tub in the back of the shop, he went to grab it , with help from Rolo, while Twix made the fire.

Roaring away, the little ones warmed up by the fire and stopped crying, thankfully, as they were making the road turn green.

The bath was placed on top of the fire and the sugar machine pumped sugar into it.

It was working!

34

'I will now make the treacle…' Humphrey knew exactly what to do. He understood that he had had a visit in his dreams by the little people in distress. They needed his help. The treacle was bubbling away, everyone was cheering.

'We need buckets,' said Humphrey.

'I have a bucket,' Poppet replied.

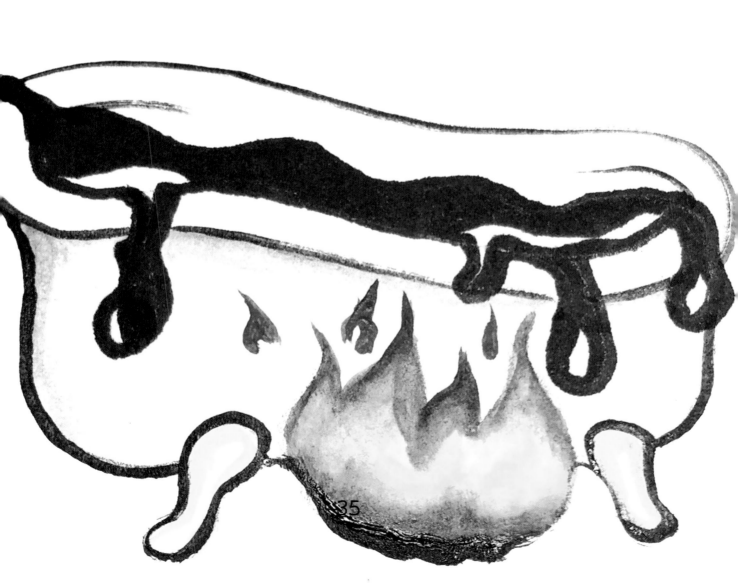

Now, the little people became very excited.

One ran up to the ship and waited for the treacle to be put back in .

One by one Rolo, Poppet, Humphrey, Twix and Mrs Spice filled the bucket and passed it to the little one to fill the engine with sweet treacle.

SLURP… SLURP… SLURP…

The engine turned. It made the most enormous, shaking, shudder.

GABOOCHER

CLUNK

Smoked fumed out of the object, but the smell was as sweet as candy.

37

Slowly, the object began to move, rising like a loaf of bread in the dented road. A large clap and roar followed from all the people in the village. It had worked. It really had worked.

The little people stared down from their ship, smiling for the first time. The ladder slowly disappeared as they shouted out 'thank you,' while still wearing their raincoats Poppet had given them. 'We are truly grateful for your help.' Waving goodbye, the door closed.

As if by magic, the road repaired itself and the villagers stood still looking up in amazement.

40

'Did that just really happen? Humphrey thought to himself.

The bath of treacle was empty and everyone laughed.

'We are hungry Humphrey, do you have any spare treacle?'

'Plenty,' Humphrey replied, 'plenty...'

The End

About the Author

Sarah Hunt is Director of Sarahsworldofbeauty training school and the health fairy clinic.

She is best know for social media and her passion for life and health.

She lives in Surrey with her husband.

Printed in Great Britain
by Amazon